DATE DUE

8-23-05		
12-13-05		
1-30-07		

Little White Dog

Laura Godwin

Illustrated by Dan Yaccarino

Hyperion Books for Children ▪ New York

Printed in Singapore

F I R S T   E D I T I O N

1 3 5 7 9 10 8 6 4 2

This book is set in 48-point and 64-point Eras Demi.
The artwork for each picture was prepared
using gouache on Arches watercolor paper.

Library of Congress Cataloging-in-Publication Data

Godwin, Laura
        Little white dog / by Laura Godwin ;
illustrated by Dan Yaccarino
—1st ed.
                p.   cm.
        Summary: One by one, a series of animals
disappears into the background,
until, with the lights turned on,
each animal searches for the next in line.
        ISBN 0-7868-0297-9 (trade)
—ISBN 0-7868-2256-2 (lib. bdg.)
        [1. Animals—Fiction.
2. Color—Fiction. 3. Stories in rhyme.]
  I. Yaccarino, Dan, ill.
  II. Title.
  PZ8.3.G5465L1   1998
[E]—dc21
97-21261

For Rachel
—L. G.

For Ralph
—D. Y.

Little White Dog
in the snow,
snow's so white

where did you go?

Little Blue Bird
in the sky,
sky's so blue

where did you fly?

Little Green Bug
on the lawn,
lawn's so green

where have you gone?

Little Brown Horse
on the track,
track's so brown

won't you come back?

Little Yellow Chick
in the hay,
hay's so yellow

won't you stay?

Little Black Cat
in the night,
night's so black—

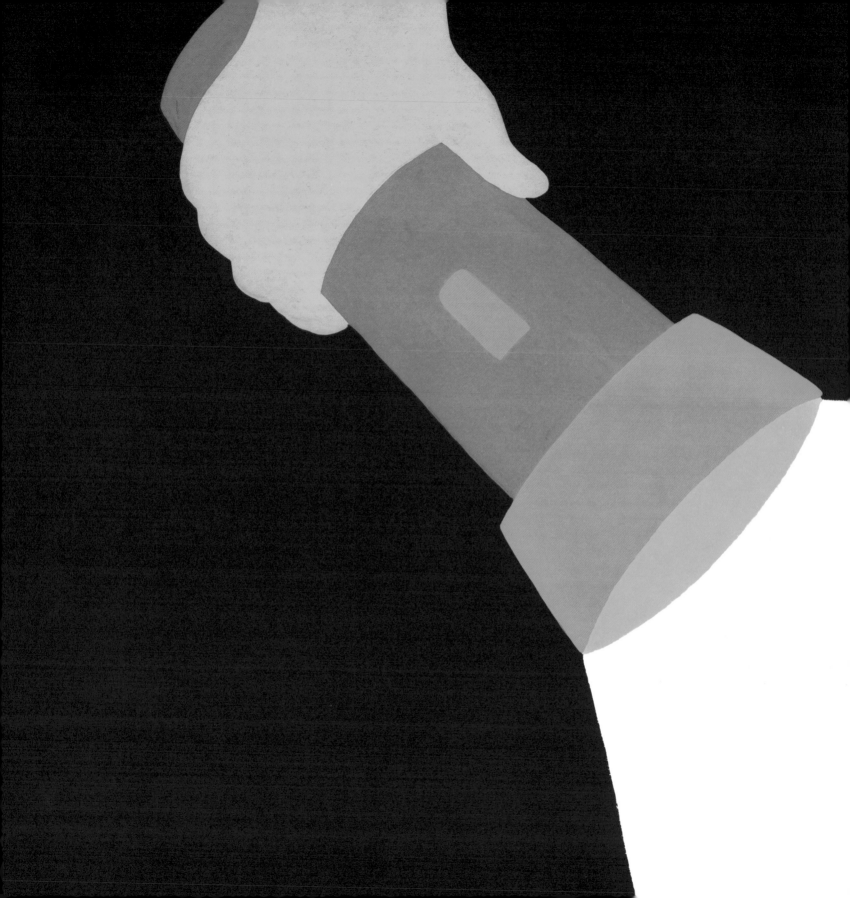

TURN ON THE LIGHT!

Turn on the light
and you will find . . .

Little Black Cat,
who went to find . . .

**Little Yellow Chick,
who went to find . . .**

Little Brown Horse,
who went to find . . .

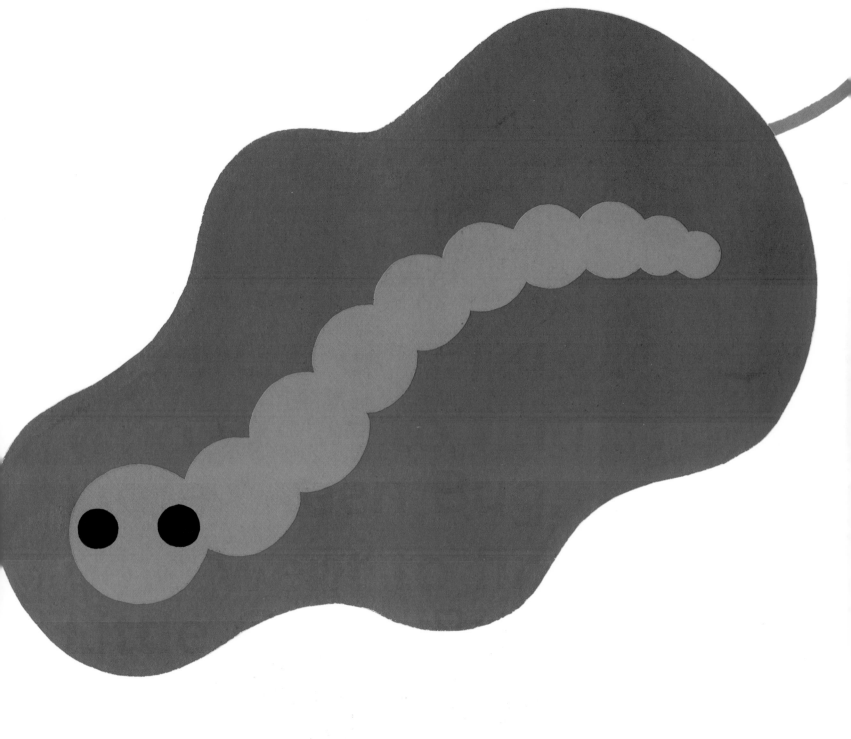

Little Green Bug,
who went to find . . .

Little Blue Bird,
who went to find . . .

Little White Dog
in the snow.

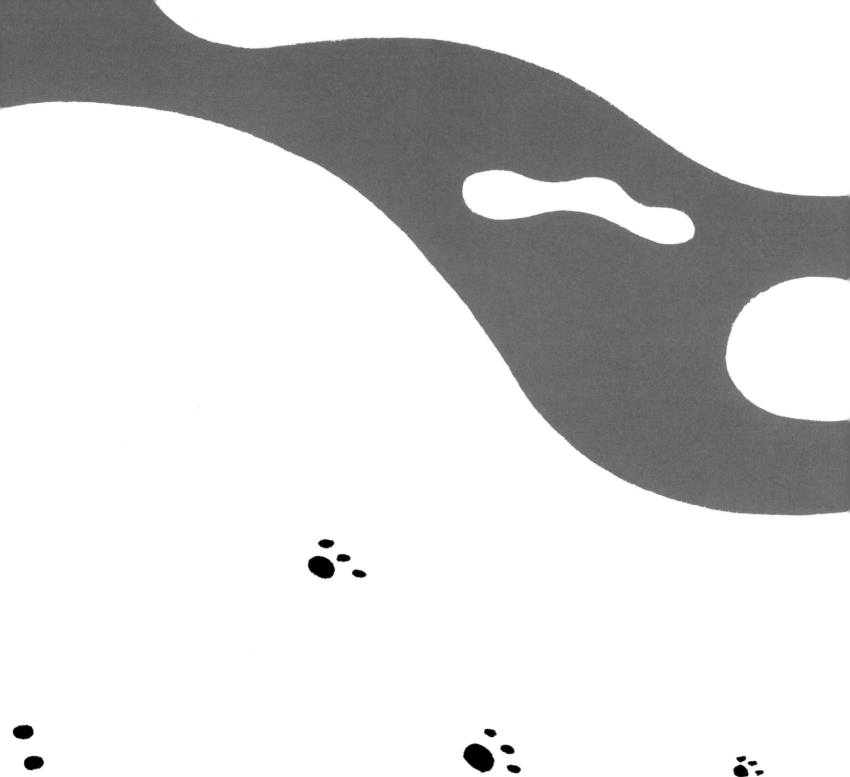